W9-AHE-369

# Martin Bear & Friends

## Books by Thomas Hauser

Non-Fiction

*Missing*

*The Trial of Patrolman Thomas Shea*

*For Our Children (with Frank Macchiarola)*

*The Family Legal Companion*

*The Black Lights: Inside the World of Professional Boxing*

*Final Warning: The Legacy of Chernobyl (with Dr. Robert Gale)*

*Muhammad Ali: His Life and Times*

*Muhammad Ali: Memories*

*Arnold Palmer: A Personal Journey*

*Confronting America's Moral Crisis (with Frank Macchiarola)*

*Muhammad Ali: In Perspective*

*Healing: A Journal of Tolerance and Understanding*

*Muhammad Ali & Company*

Fiction

*Ashworth & Palmer*

*Agatha's Friends*

*The Beethoven Conspiracy*

*Hanneman's War*

*The Fantasy*

*Dear Hannah*

*The Hawthorne Group*

For Children

*Martin Bear & Friends*

Theatre

*The Four Chords*

# Martin Bear & Friends

Thomas Hauser

Paintings by Rowena

HASTINGS HOUSE

A Division of United Publishers Group

The author acknowledges with thanks the support of Robert M. Sterling with regard to this project.

 Published in the United States by Hastings House, 50 Washington Street, Norwalk, CT 06854. 

Library of Congress Cataloging-in-Publication Data

Hauser, Thomas.
Martin Bear and friends / Thomas Hauser.
p. cm.
Summary: Martin Bear's friends show their support by helping him learn to stand on his head and to whistle and later by giving him a surprise birthday party.
ISBN 0-8038-9409-0
[1. Bears—Fiction. 2. Friendship—Fiction. 3. Stories in rhyme.] I. Title.
PZ8.3.H2875Mar 1998
[E] 97-33213
CIP
AC

Distributed by Publishers Group West

Printed in Hong Kong

10 9 8 7 6 5 4 3 2 1

**Dedication**

*For all Martin's Friends*

*People come in different shapes, sizes, and colors. Often, they have different beliefs and care about different things. But they learn to share and care about one another.*

*These tales are set in an imaginary world, very near, yet very far away. They tell of wizards, magic, dragons, dreams, all manner of strange and wonderful things—and a very special bear.*

# Contents

## Martin Bear Poems


You're Upside Down, Martin Bear 9

Why Can't You Whistle, Martin Bear? 19

Happy Birthday, Martin Bear 29

Martin Bear For President 35

Why Aren't You Playing On The Jungle Gym, Martin Bear ? 43

You're A Hero, Martin Bear 51


## Tales of Enchantment


Miles T. Penguin 59

The Magic Raccoon 65

The Nasty, Mean, Greedy, Scary Flaggapoo Monster 71

Henry The Paintbrush 77

Jonathan Gobble 83

The Little Evergreen Tree 91

# Part One

The tale of a bear who:

- tried so very hard to stand on his head
- couldn't whistle
- felt unloved and abandoned
- was much too afraid
- dreamed extraordinary dreams
- and won out in the end

Rowena

## You're Upside Down, Martin Bear

*Perseverance, dear my lord,*
*keeps honor bright.*

*William Shakespeare*

The snowdrifts had melted; the brook ice had cleared.
The bright sun stood ready for spring as it neared.
Flowers of all colors awoke in their beds,
Stretched out their arms and picked up their heads.
The cold gray skies lifted; the weather turned fair.
The March winds gave way to a breeze in the air.
"It's spring," cried the robin. "So it is," said the mole.
"Winter's gone," laughed the woodchuck as it crawled
from its hole.

"No more ice," cheered the duckling. "Goodbye snow," croaked the toad.

"It's springtime at last," the old rooster crowed.

"Hrumph, at last," said the skunk. "Hooray," buzzed the bee;

"The weather's as nice as I hoped it would be."

"Let's all have a party," said the little old hen;

"To celebrate now that it's springtime again."

"Good idea," cried the rabbit; "let's do it today."

"I've got just the spot," chirped the cagey old jay;

"Right by the farm owned by old Mister Bear,

Where the sweet smell of honeysuckle drifts through the air;

That spot on the lawn by the old maple tree

Is as ideal to party as any could be."

"Let's go," the squirrel shouted. "Follow me," said the toad;

"We'll be there in a jiffy; it's right down the road."

Cross the meadow they travelled to the edge of the farm,

Where all of a sudden they stopped in alarm.

"Hey!" cried the chipmunk. "Do you see what I see,

Right on the lawn by the old maple tree?

Someone else is there first; who's that pudgy kid there?"

"I know," said the woodchuck; "that's Martin Bear."

"Hey, Martin," they shouted; "good morning to you.

Can we party here by this tree when you're through?"

"Of course," Martin answered. "Thanks a lot," said the jay.

"Say, what are you trying to do anyway?"

"Well," answered Martin, "as some of you know,
I like to play sports but I run kind of slow.
I can't catch a thing, and I don't throw too well.
The last time I swung from a tree branch I fell.
So this morning I woke up and to myself said,
I'd like to see if I can stand on my head.
This spot on the lawn by the old maple tree
Looked as ideal to do it as any could be.
It won't take me long; t'will be easy as pie.
I've seen it in pictures; I'll do it first try.
I'll zip right on up; like an airplane I'll zoom.
Here I go now, so just watch me—". . . . CRASH, BOOM!
"Uh oh," said the chipmunk. "That wasn't so hot.
It looks like you'll have to sure practice a lot.
You didn't get up very far off the ground
Before you came down with a sickening sound."
"You're right," Martin answered. "That wasn't so good.
This could be more work than I thought it would.
This might be more tough than I thought it would be.
But I'll get it right; it's not too tough for me."
"Good luck," said the robin with a wave of its wing.
"We'd watch you, but we're off to celebrate spring.
We'll come back in June to see how you've done.
But as for right now, we're off to have fun."
"Let's go," the squirrel shouted. "Follow me," said
the toad.
"There's another good tree just a way down the road.
Martin will be here till after spring ends."
And they left him to practice without any friends.

The March days passed quickly, and soon they gave way
To the showers of April and flowers of May.
The June sun grew hot up above in the sky,
And the days passed till it was the Fourth of July.
"We have to do something," said the squirrel to the jay,
"To celebrate our independence today.
Something that's neat and will be lots of fun,
But still get us out of the blistering sun."
"I know," said the rooster. "Me too," said the bee.
Let's party down by Mister Bear's maple tree."
"Good idea," cried the rabbit. "Yes sir," said the skunk.
"We'll party all day in the shade of its trunk."
"Let's go," the squirrel shouted. "Follow me," said
the toad;
"We'll be there in a jiffy; it's right down the road."
Cross the meadow they travelled to the edge of the farm,
Where all of a sudden they stopped in alarm.
"Oh my gosh!" the hen shouted. "Do you see what I see
Right on the lawn by the old maple tree?
With sweat trickling down from his reddish-brown hair;
Right by the maple tree, Martin's still there."
"Hey Martin," they shouted; "will you tell us please,
Why you're out in the sun when it's ninety degrees?"
"Well," Martin answered, his face blushing red;
"For months I have tried to stand up on my head.
I haven't quite got it, but I'm better; you'll see.
I'm trying right now; will you root hard for me?"
"Of course," said the chipmunk. "Of course," said the jay.
"We must," said the skunk; "you are right in our way."

"Thank you," said Martin. "I'll need your support.
I'm not quite as good as I'd like to report.
But this time I'll do it; I'll start and won't stop.
This time I can do it. Just watch me—" . . . KERPLOP!
"Groan," said the rabbit. "Too bad," chirped the jay.
"I really thought Martin would do it today."
The skunk was less kindly: "He toppled; I knew it."
Said Martin, "I'll practice some more till I do it."

The summer months passed; soon the hot sun was gone.
Leaves of all colors littered the lawn.
Said the rooster, "Let's party to bring in the fall.
I've got an idea; let's all have a masked ball."
"That's great," said the robin. "Sounds fun," said
the mole.
"With costumes and dancing and good rock and roll.
Where should we have it?" "I know," said the bee.
"Right on the lawn by the old maple tree."
"Let's go," the squirrel shouted. "Follow me," said
the toad;
"We'll be there in a jiffy; it's right down the road."
Cross the meadow they travelled to the edge of the farm,
Where all of a sudden they stopped in alarm.
"Oh my gosh," said the hen. "Do you see what I see?
Poor Martin's still there by the old maple tree."
And sure enough, even though summer was gone,
Martin was still standing there on the lawn.
The crisp smell of autumn leaves blew through the air,
But right by the maple tree, Martin was there.

"I can do it," he said to himself with a sigh.
"I can stand on my head if I try and I try.
I won't give up now because quitting is junk.
I'll do it this time; yes, I'll do it—" . . . . KERPLUNK!
The animals watched from the edge of the lawn,
And as Martin fell, they turned and were gone.
"Poor Martin," the squirrel to the old rooster said.
"I wish we could help him to stand on his head.
I know he should do it himself on his own.
But gosh, I feel bad that he looks so alone."

The autumn months passed; the leaves soon all fell.
And the animals gathered for one last farewell.
"Let's have a party," the old rooster said.
"Now that it's winter and we're off to bed."
"Where should we have it?" asked the mole and the bee.
"I know," said the hen; "by the old maple tree."
"Let's go," the squirrel shouted. "Follow me," said
the toad;
"We'll be there in a jiffy; it's right down the road."
Cross the meadow they travelled to the edge of the farm,
Where all of a sudden they stopped in alarm.
"Oh no!" cried the chipmunk. "Do you see what I see;
Right over there by the old maple tree?
Winter's upon us; a chill's in the air.
But right by the maple tree, Martin's still there.
Look; he's still trying. He just will not quit.
He's got lots of spunk, we all must admit."

But as they looked on, they heard Martin say,
"I hope I can do it; today's the last day.
I've tried all year long, and I've worked at it so.
But today's the last day before it starts to snow."
"Come on," said the woodchuck. "Let's show him we care.
Let's all gather round him and cheer for that bear."
So with just one day left and his hope almost gone,
The animals gathered to cheer Martin on.
"Okay," chirped the robin. "Let's go," yelled the hen.
"We're on your side, Martin; so try it again.
Keep going; you've got it. . . . groan. . . . almost. . . . not quite. . . .
Keep trying; don't give up; and you'll get it right."
Then Martin bent over and started on up.
"He's just about made it; he's almost—" . . . . KERPLUP!
"Don't stop," the squirrel hollered. "Oh please, please don't stop.
Just keep right on trying till your feet are on top."
"I've had it," said Martin with a sad heavy sigh.
I just cannot do it, though I try and I try.
I won't ever make it, though I've worked all year through.
I guess it's just something that I'll never do."
"Try harder," they shouted. "You can do it," they cried.
"We're all for you, Martin. "We're right by your side."
"Well, all right," said Martin. "I'll try it for you.
Just one more time, though, and then I am through."

So Martin got down on his hands and his knees,
Bent his head forward and whispered, "Oh please!
Please let me make it; it's important to me
To stand on my head by this old maple tree."
Then Martin rolled forward and pushed down his head,
Gritted his teeth while his face turned bright red.
He thrust his legs out; then straight up toward the sky:
**"He's done it!"** he heard all the animals cry.
"He made it! He's done it! Look at his toes!
They're up in the air, and the ground's by his nose.
He's tried all year long, and he just would not stop.
Now his head's down below, and his feet are on top."
The crowd surged toward Martin; they whooped and they shouted.
They laughed and applauded the friend they had doubted.
Their roar echoed wide and their cheers filled the air.
"You've done it! **You're all upside down, Martin Bear!"**

Rowena

# Why Can't You Whistle, Martin Bear?

*I come from fields once tall with wheat, from pastures deep in fern and thistle; I come from vales of meadowsweet, and I love to whistle.*

—*E. B. White*

By a fast-running brook on a warm day in June,
The animals gathered to whistle a tune.
"Tweet," sang the robin. "Tweet," chirped the jay.
"Tweet," went the toad as he warbled away.
"Tweet," crooned the rabbit, the squirrel, and the bee.
Even the beaver was whistling on key.

The air filled with laughter, music, and fun.
Everyone whistled—well, not everyone.
"Hey!" cried the chipmunk. "Look over there;
Right by that tree, it's our friend Martin Bear.
But Martin's not whistling; he looks kind of grim.
What in the world is the matter with him?"
"I dunno," said the woodchuck. "I'll go check him out.
Hey, Martin," he shouted. "What's all this about?
Why aren't you whistling? What happened?
  What's wrong?
How come you aren't joining in on our song?"
"I'm tired," said Martin. "And I don't know the tune.
Besides, it's bad luck if you whistle in June.
And anyway, since it's the middle of spring,
I'm much much too busy to join you and sing."
"Nonsense," they shouted. "That's all a big lie.
Be honest and tell us the real reason why."
"Well," Martin mumbled, and he hung down his head,
As he brushed back a tear from his soft eyes and said,
"The truth is, it looks like a whole lot of fun
To whistle a tune standing out in the sun.
But some things I do in a way that's real clever,
And others I can't, though I've tried them forever.
I can find a bee's honey with a sniff of my nose,
Balance a ball on the tip of my toes,
Or roll down a hill like a lightning-fast missile.
But I've tried and I've tried and I just cannot whistle."

"Why, of course you can whistle," said the squirrel and the jay.
"It's easy as pie; why we do it each day.
Just pucker your lips; put a curl in your tongue;
And you'll whistle out as you never have sung."
"Well, all right," said Martin. "I'll do what you say.
I guess it will work if I try it your way.
I'll give it my best and, well, maybe, who knows?
I'm ready to start, so just listen, here goes"
"—P F F F T H F—"
"Uh oh," said the chipmunk, "that sure wasn't it.
All that we got was a face full of spit.
You didn't come close to a musical sound.
All that you did was spray water around."
"I know," grumbled Martin, "But what can I do?
I'd love to be able to whistle like you."
"Well," said the robin, "the truth of it is,
You don't have to be a phenomenal whiz.
There's no one who taught us; somehow we just knew it.
We don't even practice; somehow we just do it."
"Well, I can't just do it," Martin said with a sigh.
I've never been able, though I try and I try.
Isn't there something you people can do
To help me to whistle as sweetly as you?"
"I know," said the woodchuck. "There's a man from a school;
A music professor, who knows every rule.

Professor McWhiffle lives just down the street.
For sure, he'll teach Martin to whistle tweet-tweet."
"Good idea," said the rabbit. "Let's see him right now.
Professor McWhiffle will know the way how."
So off to McWhiffle's the animals sped.
And to the Professor the red rooster said,
"Hello, this is Martin, a really nice bear.
He's one of our friends, conscientious and fair.
He's funny and honest, hard-working and sweet.
He's got a bad problem; he can't go tweet-tweet."
"Hmmm," said McWhiffle, "a problem indeed.
But fear not, for I can supply what you need.
I've written a book that's a little bit long;
But from it you learn how to whistle a song."
"Great," Martin answered. "I know how to read.
In fact, I can go at a pretty good speed.
How many pages? Reading is fun."
"Well," said McWhiffle, "a million-and-one."
"Yikes," cried out Martin, "That's too much to do.
By the time that I finished, I'd be ninety-two.
I don't want to study the longest book known.
I think I'll try whistling again on my own—
"—P F F F T H F—"
"Oh my," said McWhiffle, eyes spinning around.
"What an appalling and horrible sound.
Your whistle sounds just like an elephant's yelp.
I think you had better look elsewhere for help."

"All right," Martin answered. "Does anyone know
Who else might help me or where I can go?"
"I've got an idea," said the little green toad.
"There's a very big hill just a way down the road.
On top of the hill lives a very old man.
I'm sure he'll help Martin if anyone can."
"Good idea," said the rabbit. "Let's go right away.
Maybe the old man will know what to say."
So off to the hilltop the animals sped,
And when they all got there, the red rooster said,
"Hello, Mister Man; we've a problem, you see;
Martin can't whistle; he's sad as can be.
And we were all hoping that you'd show him how.
If it's not too much trouble, could you do it right now?"
"Why, of course, I'd be glad to," the ancient man said.
"Take a brown paper bag; put it over his head.
Make him breathe in and count up one, two, three.
And Martin will whistle as sweet as can be."
"Sounds odd," said the woodchuck." "Absurd," chirped the jay.
"But Martin is desperate; we'll do what you say."
"Here's a brown bag," the very old man said.
They took it and put it on poor Martin's head.
"Help!" Martin hollered. "It's dark! I can't see.
How in the world can a brown bag help me?"
"Who knows," said the chipmunk. "Not me," said the hen.
"But it's on you, so why not try whistling again."

"All right," Martin answered. "The man claims he knows.
I'll give it my best so just listen, here goes—
"—P F F F T H F—"
"Oh, that was bad," the toad cried in dismay.
"Martin will never learn whistling this way."
"You're right," the bee grumbled. "You're right," the hen said.
"Bags are for lunch, not a little bear's head.
But what can we do? Oh, there must be a way
To teach our friend Martin to whistle today."
"I know," said the chipmunk. "By the edge of the lake
Lives a wizard who has to know what it will take.
I'm sure he can do it by casting a spell.
He's bound to have Martin Bear whistling well."
"Good idea," said the rabbit. "Let's go there real quick.
'Cause all Martin's phooeing is making me sick."
So off to the lake all the animals sped.
And as soon as they got there, the red rooster said,
"Hello, Mr. Wizard; this is Martin, our friend.
We're trying to help him; we're at our wits' end.
Poor Martin can't whistle; he's never learned how.
We'd like it if you cast a spell on him now."
"Of course," said the wizard. "T'will be easy for me.
I know spells and magic from A on through Z.
Just give him this potion I've made up to drink.
And I'll have him whistling as fast as a wink."
"Gulp," Martin said as he swallowed the brew.
"Okay, it's all gone; now please, what should I do?"

Then the wizard looked up toward the clear bright blue sky,
And chanted a spell with a fearsome loud cry.
"Oh gribble; Oh glubben; Oh gurgle; Oh glog!
Oh raindrops and lightning and thunder and fog!
Oh hocus; Oh pocus; Oh smiggledybissel!
Oh make this poor little bear able to whistle."
The wizard threw up both his hands toward the sky.
Lightning and thunderbolts crashed up on high.
"All right," he told Martin. "It's happened; I knew it.
It's time now to whistle; I want you to do it."—
"—P F F F T H F—"
"Drats!" cried the wizard. "You did it all wrong.
You'll *never* be able to whistle a song.
Leave right this minute, before I get mad.
You'll never be able to whistle; too bad."
"Hey," cried the chipmunk. "Watch what you say.
"You'll hurt our friend's feelings by talking that way.
You're a silly old wizard; you're no help at all;
So hocus your pocus and smiggle your ball."
Then the animals turned and walked off with their friend.
"Well," Martin said, "I guess this is the end.
You've all been real nice, and you've tried all day long.
But I'll never be able to whistle a song."
"So what," said the woodchuck. "It's not a big thing.
"You don't have to whistle to join when we sing.
From now on, whenever we whistle a song,
We'd like you to help us by humming along."

"That's right," said the rabbit, "and please please don't worry.
There's no need to whistle in such a big hurry.
You're trying too hard; you're all nervous and tight.
Relax, take it easy, and you'll get it right.
Maybe not now; but we're certain, someday.
And do it or not, you're our friend anyway."
"Thank you," said Martin. "That makes me feel good.
I've been more concerned and upset than I should.
But someday I'll learn how to whistle real sweet.
And then I'll be able to go *tweedle-tweet*."
"Omigosh!" said the beaver. "Omigosh!" said the hen.
"Omigosh!" said the rooster. "You did it just then."
"Omigosh!" said the duckling, the squirrel, and the jay.
"That's the sweetest darn whistle we've heard all today."
"*Tweet-tweet*," went Martin. "Look! I did it once more.
*Tweedledy-tweet!* That's as good as before.
*Tweedledy-tweedledy-tweedledy-twee!*
That's the prettiest sound in the whole world to me."
The animals cheered and broke out in a song.
Martin joined in, and they whistled along.
And that's a good note for the end of this poem.
Martin Bear whistling his happy way home.

Birthday
Rowena

# Happy Birthday, Martin Bear

*Sad? Why should I be sad? It's my birthday. The happiest day of the year.*

*—A. A. Milne*

The day was just starting; the sky barely light.
The bright golden sun wasn't even in sight.
But, wide awake, Martin was lying in bed,
With wonderful thoughts spinning round in his head.
"Today is my birthday," he thought with a smile.
"I knew it would come, but it sure took a while.
Sometimes I thought it would never get here,
But now it's the very best day of the year.
I know I'll get presents like books and balloons,
And CDs with some of my favorite tunes.
There'll be ice cream and cookies to help celebrate.
I'm so very excited I hardly can wait."

Slowly the seconds and minutes ticked by.
The sun lifted up to the edge of the sky.
The alarm clock went off; Martin jumped out of bed;
Put on his clothes, and then eagerly said,
"Time to get started; I'm ready to go.
I wonder if anyone ever could know
How I've waited all year for this one special day?
I can't wait to hear what my parents will say."
Down to the kitchen, the little bear ran.
His mother was scrambling some eggs in a pan.
His father was reading the paper for news.
Martin looked down at the top of his shoes.
"I'm waiting," he thought, "to hear what they say.
For surely, they both know that today's the big day.
They have to say something; I'm another year old."
"Eat your eggs," said his mother, "before they get cold."
Somberly, Martin looked down at his plate.
"For sure, they'll say something," he thought as he ate.
But his father kept reading with nary a blink;
And his mother began putting plates in the sink.
"Are you finished?" she asked when the eggs were
all gone.
"Don't be late for school; you had best run along."
"All right," Martin answered, "I'll be on my way.
But don't you have anything special to say?"
"No," said his mother. "No," said his dad.
"Gosh," Martin whispered, "that makes me feel sad.
But I know for certain it won't be this way
At school, where my friends will remember the day."

So off to the schoolhouse the little bear sped,
And with every footstep he eagerly said,
"Today is my birthday; at long last it's here;
The happiest, very best day of the year.
I've waited so long for this one special day.
I can't wait to hear what my friends will all say."
The classroom was open when Martin got there.
He went to his desk and sat down in his chair.
"I'm waiting," he thought as he looked at the floor.
"But I really don't think I can wait anymore."
"All right," said the teacher; "now everyone's here.
But before I start teaching, I want a big cheer."
"Oh boy," Martin whispered. "She didn't forget.
This will for sure be the best moment yet."
"I want a big cheer," said the teacher once more.
"For Mr. Lavelli—the school janitor.
He's washed all the windows; they're so bright and clear.
Let's shout out hooray loud enough so he'll hear."
"Hooray!" the kids shouted with voices raised high.
"Mr. Lavelli's a wonderful guy.
The windows look great; he sure did his job well."
Poor Martin just sat there; he wanted to yell:
"Hey, all you people; how can this be?
Don't you all know what this day means to me?
Today is my birthday; can't somebody say,
'Happy birthday, dear Martin, please have a good day.'"
The lessons began; Martin quietly sat
Through reading and writing and math and all that;

Through history, science and painting and gym;
But none of his friends said a darn thing to him.
Then the school bell rang out, and his classes were done.
"At last," Martin thought; "maybe now I'll have fun."
But all of his friends were too busy to play,
And everyone seemed to be running away.
"Please play," he pleaded. "Oh, please, don't say no."
"Sorry," they said. "We have someplace to go."
Then his friends all ran off, leaving poor Martin there;
A very forlorn, very unhappy bear.
"Oh golly," he said with a sad heavy sigh.
"I really feel bad; I could sit down and cry.
But my grandma and grandpa would never forget.
I'll go visit them; then I'll be less upset."
So off to his grandparents the little bear ran.
"I'll get there," he thought, "just as fast as I can,
'Cause Grandma and Grandpa will surely both say,
'Martin, we love you; today's the big day.'"
But, wouldn't you know, Martin got to their house;
And no one was stirring; not even a mouse.
The front door was locked; there was nobody there.
"They're gone," Martin whispered. "There's no one to care.
No one remembered; I'm ready to cry.
But I won't; no, I won't; and I'll tell you just why.
I won't cry at all 'cause today's the big day.
Now I'm too old to cry—that's what I say."
Biting his lip, Martin turned on that note
And started toward home with a lump in his throat.

"I won't cry," he whispered. "I'm gonna be strong.
But no one remembered, and gosh that was wrong."
When Martin got home, it nearly was night.
His house was all dark, and the door was shut tight.
He opened it up and trudged on inside.
"Psst!" said a voice. "He's here; quick, let's hide."
"Hey," Martin wondered. "Who could that be?
I'll put on a light, and then maybe I'll see."
He reached for the switch, and then came the cries
From his family and friends, who all shouted,
"SURPRISE!"
"Omigosh!" Martin hollered. "You didn't forget.
But you wouldn't believe it; I've been so upset.
And now I'm so happy I hardly can say
How so very special you've made this whole day."
Then they had a big party with lots of balloons,
And everyone sang Martin Bear's favorite tunes.
They gave him great presents; boy, was it fun.
And when all the merriment almost was done,
His mother and father brought out a huge cake
So big it had taken ten hours to bake.
Its insides were chocolate; the frosting was white.
Martin just stared; what a beautiful sight.
And right on its top, spelled in sugar it said
The very best message he ever had read:

We love you a lot,
and all of us care;
Happy Birthday to you,
with our love, Martin Bear.

MARTIN
FOR
PRESIDENT
MARTIN
FOR
PRESIDENT
Rowena

# Martin Bear For President

*There is bound to be a certain amount of trouble*
*running any country.*
*If you are President, the trouble happens to you.*

*—Donald Marquis*

Martin was lying in bed warm and tight,
When his parents came in to kiss him goodnight.
"Sleep well," his dad told him. "You're a wonderful boy.
We love you a lot; you're our pride and our joy.
You help out at home, and you work hard in school.
Your friends say you practice that old golden rule.
Your mother and I are so proud when we see
What you've become and what you can be."

"Thanks," Martin told them. "I love you both too.
It's great to have parents as super as you."
Then they bent down to kiss him and turned off the light,
Leaving Martin alone in his bed in the night.
"But what can I be?" Martin wondered out loud
As he drifted away on a sleepy white cloud.
"What will I do when I'm grown up and work?
Will I be a doctor, an artist, or clerk;
A teacher, a plumber, a salesman, a judge;
Or maybe a chef who makes fabulous fudge?"
And then something happened; Martin didn't know why.
But a lightning bolt flashed up above in the sky.
And suddenly as he lay sleeping in bed,
A perfect idea jumped right into his head.
"Fantastic!" he shouted. "I know what I'll be.
**President**—that's just the right job for me."
He opened his eyes and looked up at the sun.
The nighttime had fled; a new day had begun.
And right at that moment, right then, and right there;
The campaign trail started for candidate bear.
He packed up his suitcase and left his warm home,
Saying, "I'll meet the voters from Texas to Nome.
I'll start in New Hampshire and work my way west,
Till all of my countrymen know I'm the best.
I'll shake hands, give speeches, and enter debates,
Like Kennedy, Lincoln, and other past greats.

And come next November, when the votes are all cast,
This country will have me as President at last."
As the campaign got started, the pollsters all sniggered.
"There's no way that Martin can win," they all figured.
But out on the hustings, twelve hours a day,
Martin was busily working away.
The more he kept at it, the more folks he met.
And people said, "Martin's the best candidate yet."
"Why?" asked the pollsters. "What has he got?
What's it about Martin that makes him so hot?"
"Well," said the voters, "that's not easy to say.
But, as long as you asked, let us put it this way—
We want a leader who cares and is just;
A man we can count on; a man we can trust;
One who is noble and honest and fair;
We want a good man; we want Martin Bear."

The primaries passed; the conventions began.
Martin kept running; he ran and he ran.
One party caucused and made known its choice.
He had a long nose, and he drove a Rolls Royce.
He didn't like children; he'd lie and he'd cheat.
But as a campaigner, he'd be tough to beat.
Then the other side met in a big conference hall,
With thousands of people who stretched wall to wall,
To listen to speeches in the hope that they might
Choose someone who'd go out and do the job right.

"I'd like to be President," Martin told those who'd listen.
"I can supply what America's missin'."
At first, no one gave him a ghost of a chance.
Someone else had a big lead in advance.
And since people knew Martin's hopes were real slim,
None of the delegates voted for him.
But as the convention dragged on through the night,
Martin's prediction turned out to be right.
A man from Virginia and one from Nebraska,
A woman from Kansas and three from Alaska,
Folks from the east and folks from the west,
Started to think Martin Bear was the best.
Then a tall man stood up in a long coal-black coat,
And said he was going to give Martin his vote.
And suddenly down on the convention floor,
All of the delegates started to roar,
"We want a leader who cares and is just;
A man we can count on; a man we can trust;
One who is noble and honest and fair;
We want a good man; we want Martin Bear."
The will of the people could not be ignored.
Martin's vote total rose up till it soared.
And soon by a vote that approached acclamation,
Martin was given the top nomination.

The campaign that followed was bitter and tough.
The other side fought hard, and boy were they rough.
But Martin kept at it for week after week,
And people would listen whenever he'd speak.

He talked about freedom and safe streets at night,
The need to restore our armed services' might,
Full rights for women and minority classes,
Good jobs for all of America's masses.
And when in November the ballots were counted,
Martin's vote total just mounted and mounted,
Until by a margin incredibly wide,
The tally became an electoral landslide.
"He won," people cheered; "and it's good for the nation;
The most wonderful day since our country's creation.
All we need now is a big celebration,
And that will come soon at the inauguration."
And so by the hundreds of thousands they went
To see Martin sworn in as their President.
And as he took office with a tear in his eye,
All of America started to cry—
"We have a leader who cares and is just;
A man we can count on; a man we can trust;
One who is noble and honest and fair;
We have a good man; we have Martin Bear."

T'would be nice if the story could end on that note,
With America cheering its election vote.
But the Presidency takes a lot more than resolve;
The problems aren't simple or easy to solve.
Martin worked hard both at day and at night,
Trying his darnedest to do the job right.
But it took up more time than he thought it would take.
And now and then Martin would make a mistake.

Soon people noticed the economy was down,
And Martin's supporters were starting to frown.
Congress turned down his defense bill request,
Saying that they and not Martin knew best.
Foreign affairs and minority rights
Turned into endless political fights.
And then when things turned particularly bad,
Even his mother and father got mad.
"Martin," they scolded, "we've told you before
Not to leave clothes and your toys on the floor.
Clean up your messy room, now on the double;
Or else, Mr. President, you're in big trouble."
"I can't," Martin answered. "I'm already late
For a meeting with my Secretary of State."
"No excuses," they told him. "Your room's a sad sight.
Clean it up now, or no TV tonight."
The next day in school, things became even sadder.
Martin's parents were mad, but his teacher was madder.
"Mr. President," she scolded, "as of this date,
All of your lessons and homework are late.
I don't understand, you were once such a joy.
But now you've become an impossible boy."
"I'm sorry," said Martin, "but I'm behind in my readers,
'Cause all week I've been with Congressional leaders."
"No excuses," she chided. "If this is a sample,
Your behavior is setting a tragic example."
At the end of the class, Martin's friends stopped to say,
"We're off to the park; will you join us to play?"

"I can't," answered Martin. "For the next hour and a half,
I have to sit down with the Joint Chiefs of Staff."
"Too bad," they all told him. "We're going to play ball.
I guess being President's no fun at all."
And as they ran off, Martin simply sat there;
A miserable, lonely, and unhappy bear.
"Gosh, I feel sad," he said with a sigh.
And then the tears fell as he started to cry.
"Help," he sobbed softly. "Won't someone help me?
Being President's not what I thought it would be.
Help," he said louder. Then he started to shout.
"Help me; oh help me; oh help, I want out!"
He'd never been sadder; he cried and he cried.
He wished he could run from it all and just hide.
And then—FLASH—CRACK—ZOOM—he was back in his bed,
Looking at both of his parents, who said,
*"Martin, stop crying; things aren't like they seem.*
*Martin, please wake up; it's only a dream."*
Rubbing the sleep from his soft little eyes,
Martin sat up and began to realize
That it was still night; he was still in his bed.
The entire campaign had been all in his head.
"Boy," he said softly; "that really was frightening.
But I guess it was also a little enlightening.
'Cause the one thing I've learned is in any event,
At my age, I don't want to be President."

# Why Aren't You Playing On The Jungle Gym, Martin Bear?

*Courage is resistance to fear, mastery of fear;*
*not absence of fear.*

*—Mark Twain*

The playground was full after school every day,
When all of the animals gathered to play.
They'd build in the sandbox; they'd see-saw and swing.
They'd slide on the slide; they'd laugh and they'd sing.
They'd run through the sprinkler and get
themselves wet.
They'd race back and forth like a lightning-fast jet.
They'd skip and they'd jump; they'd play hopscotch
and ball.
But one of the games was their favorite of all.

"The jungle gym's best," said the squirrel and the bee.
"Up at the top, look how far you can see."
"The jungle gym's best," said the rabbit and hen.
"We climb it again and again and again."
"The jungle gym's best," said the shiny red rooster.
"When I come to the park, I'm a jungle gym booster."
"The jungle gym's best," said the woodchuck and jay.
"We could play on it twenty-four hours a day."
The robin and duckling agreed with the rest.
Both thought the jungle gym really was best.
The chipmunk and toad had the very same view;
But one of the animals differed—guess who?
While all of his friends climbed on up toward the sky,
Martin Bear sat on a bench right nearby.
He looked kind of sad; he said hardly a word.
And the few thoughts he whispered, nobody heard.
"I'm frightened," he said in a voice that was low.
"If I tried it, I'd fall off; I'm certain, I know.
My hands would get sweaty; I'd loosen my grip.
The bar would get caught on my stomach or hip.
My shoelaces would happen to come all untied;
Or my legs would get wobbly; I'd slip and I'd slide.
I'd fall to the ground with a crash and a smack
On top of my head or my face or my back.
I wish I weren't frightened; I'd give it a try.
But I'm too scared to climb up on anything high.
Just the thought of that height makes me shiver
and shake.
And the thought of a fall makes me quiver and quake."

The animals played until late in the day.
Then, laughing and singing, they all ran away.
All except Martin—who sat all alone,
With the saddest sensation he ever had known.
"I wish I could climb," Martin said with a sigh.
"I want to so much that I'm ready to cry.
I want to so much, but the truth of it all
Is the jungle gym's big, and I'm scared of a fall."
So day after day, Martin sat in the shade
Of the jungle gym while all the animals played.
He'd wish and he'd hope for the courage to try,
But was always afraid to climb up toward the sky.
Then one afternoon, when the day was near done
And the horizon was touched by the edge of the sun,
Something happened that Martin had hoped for all day.
The squirrel and the chipmunk came over to say,
"Hey, Martin; we've noticed when all of us climb
On the jungle gym, you stay away every time.
And we were just thinking that maybe you might
Like a lesson in climbing up jungle gyms right."
Martin's heart fluttered and skipped past a beat.
A shudder went down from his head to his feet.
This was the time; his big chance now was here,
To beat back the shivers and conquer his fear.
"Well," he said slowly, "as both of you guessed,
At jungle gym climbing I'm hardly the best.
The jungle gym's big, and I'm not very tall.
The truth of it is, I'm afraid of a fall."

"Don't worry," they told him. "It's not hard to do.
The first time we tried, we were both frightened too.
Just take your time climbing, and hold each bar tight.
Try not to be nervous, and you'll get it right."
"I don't know," Martin said. "I'm afraid and I'm scared.
You're asking for something that I've never dared.
You say I can do it, but what if I don't?
What if I fall?"—Said the chipmunk, "You won't."
So Martin went over and touched the first bar.
"It's slippery," he said, "and the top is too far.
It's way too high up, and I'm frightened of heights.
The sky is for eagles and airplanes and kites.
The sky is for clouds and for people who dare;
But the sky is most certainly not for a bear."
"All right," said the chipmunk, "don't go to the top.
Just climb up one level, and then you can stop.
Just climb the first bar, and we'll see how you feel.
The first bar is easy; it's not a big deal."
"Gulp," Martin said. "Well, I guess that's all right.
The top is too far, but the first bar I might—
Maybe I—maybe I—maybe I would
Climb up one level, if you thought that I could."
"Of course you can do it," the squirrel said out loud.
"Climb up one level, and make yourself proud."
"All right," Martin answered. "I'll try it; here goes.
But my stomach is down by the tip of my toes."
Then carefully, slowly, and worried to death,
Martin reached upward and took a deep breath.

He pulled himself up a few feet off the ground.
"I made it," he shouted out, looking around.
"I made it; I've done it; now what should I do?"
Said the chipmunk and squirrel, "Now try bar number two."
"Gulp," Martin said. "That's a little too high.
But I've done it this far, so I'll give it a try."
"That's the spirit," they told him. "You'll make it; we're sure.
Just climb level two like you climbed one before."
"All right," Martin answered, "I'm ready to do it."
Then he climbed level two—Said the chipmunk, "I knew it.
I knew he could make it; I'm as pleased as can be."
"Okay," cried the squirrel, "now let's do level three."
"I don't know," Martin answered. "I'm less scared than before,
But three is high up."—Cried the chipmunk, "One more!
Just one more level; you're doing so well."
Said Martin, "I'd like to, but what if I fell?"
"You won't," the squirrel hollered. "Take it careful and slow.
You'll make it to three; we're both certain; we know."
"All right, Martin answered. "Keep a close eye on me."
Then carefully, slowly, he climbed up to three.
"Hooray," cried the chipmunk. "Now you know how it's done.
Sometimes it's scary, but sometimes it's fun."
"You're right," Martin answered. "I'm not gonna stop.
I plan to keep climbing till I get to the top."

So, carefully, Martin climbed up to bar four.
"Fantastic! It's super; I'm going one more.
There's just one more level to the top rung and then
I'll never be frightened of climbing again."
So Martin reached up for the bar near the sky
That minutes before had seemed terribly high.
He pulled himself up without trembling or fear.
"I did it!" he shouted. "It's super up here.
It's great; it's the best; and I owe it to you.
You helped me believe it was something I'd do.
Without your support I would never have tried.
You helped me to feel I could do it inside."

Now some folks might think that this story is done.
Martin Bear battled his fears, and he won.
But the very last chapter has yet to be told;
So read on and watch Martin's story unfold.
After he learned from his friends how to climb,
He went up the jungle gym time after time.
He'd play on the bars several hours a day,
Along with the chipmunk, the squirrel, and the jay.
Soon he was climbing as well as the rest.
Said the rabbit and hen, "Martin's one of the best."
The robin and woodchuck just had to agree.
So did the rooster, the duck, and the bee.
Then one afternoon when the day was near done
And the horizon was touched by the edge of the sun,

Martin was climbing on up toward the sky,
When he happened to see the mole sitting nearby.
The mole was real quiet; it sat all alone.
Its face had a sadness that Martin had known.
And then Martin realized that not even one time
Had anyone ever seen Mr. Mole climb.
"Mr. Mole," Martin shouted, "Is it true that you might
Like a lesson in climbing up jungle gyms right?"
The mole started trembling; its heart skipped a beat;
And a shudder went down from its head to its feet.
Then at last the mole answered, "The jungle gym's tall;
And the truth of it is, I'm afraid of a fall."
"Don't be scared," Martin told him. "It's not hard to do.
The first time I tried, I was frightened like you.
Just take your time climbing and hold each bar tight.
Try not to be nervous, and you'll get it right."
"I don't know," the mole said. "I'm afraid, and I'm scared.
You're asking for something that I've never dared.
You say I can do it, but what if I don't?
What if I fall?"—Said Martin, "You won't.
You can do it; I promise; and I'll show you how.
Let's get started; I'll give you your first lesson now.
Just climb the first bar, and we'll see how you feel.
The first bar is easy; it's not a big deal.
You don't have to go all the way to the top.
Just climb up one level, and then you can stop."
"Gulp," the mole answered. "Well, I guess that's all right.
The top is too far, but the first bar I might . . . ."

Rowena

# You're A Hero, Martin Bear

*You know, this baseball game of ours comes up from the youth. Some people think, if you give them a football or something like that, naturally they're athletes right away. But you can't do that in baseball. You've got to start way down at the bottom, when you're six or seven years old. You can't wait until you're fifteen or sixteen. You've got to let it grow up with you. And if you're successful and you try hard enough, you're bound to come out on top.*

*—Babe Ruth*

Each Sunday at noon from mid-March through the fall,
Martin would take out his bat and his ball.
He'd pitch and he'd catch and he'd hit and he'd run,
Playing baseball for hours on end, having fun.

He wasn't particularly good when he hit.
Fly balls and grounders eluded his mitt.
Running the bases, he went kind of slow;
But he played with a passion that all children know.
"I love to play baseball," he'd tell all his friends.
"I'm sorry whenever the afternoon ends.
I'm fonder of baseball than eating ice cream.
I just wish that I was more help to the team.
The chipmunk, the robin, the squirrel and the bee
Are certainly all faster runners than me.
The skunk and the rooster at bat are real fine;
They hit the ball farther than me every time.
The toad and the mole and the duck and the hen
Out-catch me again and again and again.
I can't pitch as well as the rabbit and jay;
But no one tries harder than me every day."
Sometimes the animals played pick-up games.
They'd take turns as captain and call out the names
Of who was on which team and whether they'd play
Pitcher or infield or outfield that day.
But one game was special—at the end of each year,
All of the neighbors would gather to cheer
For the animal team as it went out to play
A team called The Meanies from a town far away.
"Oh boy, I'm excited," thought Martin that day.
"This is the game that I've waited to play.
This is the moment that I've waited for.
I just hope we come out ahead in the score.

At night in my bed when I'm sleeping, I dream
Of airplanes and toys and balloons and ice cream;
Of movies and hot dogs and growing real tall;
But winning this game is my best dream of all."
The animals gathered at noon set to play.
The skunk was the captain; t'was its turn that day.
"All right," the skunk ordered. "The robin and bee
Will play in the outfield alongside of me.
The chipmunk will catch, and the rabbit will pitch.
At first base, the toad and the rooster will switch.
The mole and the duckling, the hen, squirrel, and jay
Will take turns at playing the infield today.
This game is important; we'll win it; you'll see."
"Hey," hollered Martin. "What about me?"
"Oh, you," said the skunk in a voice that was gruff.
"Martin, I'm sorry; you're not good enough.
Winning's important, and losing's a taint.
We want the best players, and Babe Ruth you ain't."
"Please!" Martin pleaded. "Please, please let me play.
I've spent all year dreaming of playing today.
Please let me play, and I'll never forget it.
Please let me play, and you'll never regret it."
"Sorry," the skunk said again with a sneer.
"We don't plan on losing this game 'cause you're here.
We want our best players; not someone who'll botch it."
"All right," Martin whispered; "I'll sit down and watch it."
So Martin sat down while the others all played.
He cheered for the good plays that each of them made.

But deep down he hurt, and he had to keep trying
To smile outside, when his insides were crying.
The game was exciting; The Meanies were good.
The animals played the best baseball they could.
They hit hard and caught well and ran very fast.
The innings passed by till they came to the last.
The animals led by a score of one run.
They needed three outs and the game would be won.
The crowd was excited; the time was near, when
The game would be over—But suddenly then—
"Hey," said the chipmunk to the mole and the bee,
"I've been thinking, and something is bothering me.
Look at poor Martin, just sitting back there.
He hasn't played yet, and it's really not fair.
Martin loves baseball; he's one of our friends.
He really should play in this game 'fore it ends."
"That's right," said the robin. "That's right," said the jay.
"Martin's entitled to play ball today."
"That's right," said the squirrel and the rabbit and hen.
"That's right," said the rooster—But suddenly then—
"No way," snapped the skunk. "I'm the captain today.
"There's no way that Martin is going to play.
This game is important, and Martin will blow it.
Martin will goof up; I'm certain, I know it."
"So what," said the duckling. "Big deal," said the bee.
"Martin has feelings; that's important to me.
Not letting Martin play baseball is wrong.
Let's let him play now, 'cause we've waited too long."

"No way!" the skunk shouted. "If you do that, I'll quit."
"Goodbye," said the squirrel; "we won't miss you a bit.
Martin will play; you can like it or not.
From now on, the outfield is Martin Bear's spot."
So the skunk stomped off mad, while the animals jeered.
Then Martin stood up, and the animals cheered.
"Hooray," cried the robin. "Hooray," cried the jay.
"Three more outs," cried the toad, "and we're
winners today."
The rabbit was pitching; he threw in the ball.
"It's a pop-up; I've got it," came the rooster's clear call.
"Two more outs," cried the chipmunk. "Two more outs,
and we've won."
The next batter missed on three strikes—"Now it's one!"
"One more out," cried the duckling. "One more out,"
cried the bee.
"One more out," cried the toad, "and the whole world
will see."
"One more out," cried the rooster, the mole, and the hen.
"One more out," cried the rabbit—But suddenly then—
The next Meanie batter smashed a fearsome base hit.
"Uh oh," said the robin. "I'm worried a bit."
After that, the mole erred on an easy ground ball;
And chasing a fly, the toad happened to fall.
Now the bases were loaded and two men were out;
And all of the animals started to shout,
"One more out and we win; we're ahead by one run.
But if The Meanies can get one more hit, then
we're done.

If The Meanies can get one more hit, then we're through.
What in the world are we going to do?"

Now The Meanies' best hitter was up at the plate.

His teeth were all clenched and his eyes full of hate.

He smashed the first pitch just as hard as he could.

He smashed it real hard, and he smashed it real good.

Martin's heart trembled; his feet felt like lead.

The baseball was soaring way over his head.

If it fell to the ground, his whole team would be done.

Martin turned 'round, and he started to run.

He ran just as fast as he possibly could.

He ran just as fast as a bear ever would.

He ran for the ball in the air up above.

He ran and he ran, and he thrust out his glove.

The crowd held its breath; and who would have thought it.

The baseball came down—and Martin Bear caught it.

The ballgame was over; and by one tiny run,

Thanks to Martin Bear's catch, the animals won.

People remember that catch to this day.

And Martin remembers how his friends let him play.

Tales of:

- a penguin who spent most of his time thinking
- a magic raccoon
- an extremely unpleasant monster
- a paintbrush who yearned to be important
- a turkey with pride
- and a little evergreen tree

Rowena

# Miles T. Penguin

*If a man does not keep pace with his companions, perhaps it is because he hears a different drummer. Let him step to the music which he hears, however measured or far away.*

*—Henry David Thoreau*

It was cold in Antarctica. It was cold and the penguins were always outside, but the weather never seemed to bother them. The sun would shine for days on end. For weeks at a time, it was night. And through it all, the penguins played in the ice and snow.

Antarctica was their home. It was a world of crystal cliffs, glaciers, and frozen seas at the southernmost tip of the globe. All but a few patches of land were covered by ice two miles thick and hundreds of miles long. Travelling by land, the penguins would waddle upright or toboggan on their stomachs propelled by hind legs across the ice and snow. At sea, they were strong swimmers, breaking the surface every few strokes for a breath of air. It was in the ocean that the penguins found their food—tiny crabs less than an inch long. But it was also in the ocean that most penguins met their doom: battered by waves, crushed by ice, or eaten by ugly leopard seals.

Leopard seals were the penguins' deadliest enemy. Fully grown, they were twelve feet long and weighed eight hundred pounds. On land, the penguins were faster. But in the water, the leopard seals had more speed and far more power. Penguin children were all taught not to play in the ocean. If they did, a leopard seal might slither into the water without a sound. And then it would be too late—the penguin children would be eaten up—gone.

Every day after their morning meal, the penguin children played in the snow. Sometimes they'd make snowmen and snowpenguins, or slide on their stomachs like sleds across the icy land. Other times, they'd build snowforts, choose up sides, and throw snowballs back and forth through the air.

But Miles T. Penguin never joined them. While the others played, Miles would sit and watch. He was quite content and very happy. Often, the other children would ask, "Do you want to play with us, Miles?" But Miles would always answer, "Not now, thank you. I'm busy thinking. Maybe later."

The penguin children liked Miles. He was very quiet and very shy, but a nice penguin. They wished Miles would play with them, so they could get to know him better. But Miles liked doing things alone, watching and thinking. Each day, he'd walk with the other children to wherever they were going to play. And then, very satisfied and content, while the others played, he'd sit and think and watch alone.

One sunny morning, beneath a particularly blue sky, the penguin children decided to go near the ocean to play. An old log had washed ashore, and they decided it would make a wonderful bridge between two piles of snow. Pulling hard, they carried the log to the foot of a glacier near the water and began to build.

Miles sat, watching and thinking.

"What are you always thinking about?" one of the penguin children asked.

"Oh, lots of things," Miles answered.

"Do you want to come play with us today?"

"Not now, but maybe later; thank you."

The penguin children built two big piles of snow. Then they lifted the log up and balanced it with one end of the log on each pile.

"Now we have a bridge," they shouted.

And, one-by-one, they began to walk across it.

CRACK!

Something popped. . . . But the penguin children were too busy having fun to notice.

CRACK!

There it was again. This time, they heard it. But it wasn't the log. . . . What was it?

CRACK! CRACK! CRACK!

Miles heard the popping and ran toward the other children. "The ice is cracking," he shouted. "The ice is cracking! Run!"

But it was too late. The edge of the glacier where the children were playing had broken away. It had come apart from the rest of the ice and begun to drift out to sea.

"Help!" the penguin children shouted. "Help! Help! What can we do?"

None of them had ever been as frightened before. They were marooned on a sheet of ice that was floating away. None of them would ever be able to go home again.

Maybe they could swim to shore. That was it! They'd jump off the ice into the ocean and swim.

Miles walked to the edge of the ice and looked into the ocean. The ugly black snout of a leopard seal lay just beneath the surface of the water.

"We can't swim," he told the other penguins. "There's a leopard seal down there that will eat us all."

"Oh!" the penguin children shouted. "What are we going to do? If we go in the water, we'll be eaten alive. If we stay on the ice, we'll float out to sea and be lost forever. Oh, somebody, help! What are we going to do?"

Miles sat down near the edge of the ice, and looked out at the ocean.

"I've been thinking," he told the penguin children. "And I've thought of something to do."

"Help us, Miles. We'll do anything you say we should do."

"Well," Miles said slowly. "It seems to me that the piles of snow and log you've been playing with could be quite useful. I've watched you make snowpenguins and snowmen before. Sometimes I've even seen you make an entire fort out of ice and snow. Let's take the snow and build a snowboat. The ocean is cold and, if we make the boat thick enough, the snow will turn to ice in the water. Then we can use the log as an oar and row safely back to shore."

"Miles, you're a genius," the penguin children shouted.

"Thank you for the compliment," Miles told them.

So very quickly, the penguin children went to work. They took the two big piles of snow and packed them hard into the shape of a boat. Then they hollowed out a place where they could sit, and put the log inside. They carried the boat to the edge of the ice, and set out to sea, rowing very hard.

"Pull," they shouted. "Pull hard on the oar."

The leopard seal circled in the water nearby.

"Pull hard! We absolutely have to make it ashore"

Their home on land seemed to be growing closer.

"Pull! . . . We're almost there. . . . Pull! . . . A little more. . . . Pull! . . . Pull! . . . At last. . . . Hooray! . . . We've made it ashore."

Cheering, the penguins rushed out of the boat onto safe ground. They were home—and delighted to be there.

They were very happy that Miles was their friend. They were very glad that they had always respected his right to think and be alone. And most of all, they were thankful that Miles was so good at watching and thinking while he sat in the ice and snow.

Rowena

# The Magic Raccoon

*The vast marvel is to be alive. We dance with rapture that we should be part of the living cosmos. I am part of the sun as my eye is part of me. I am part of the earth, and my blood is part of the sea. In my very own self, I am part of my family.*

*—D. H. Lawrence*

Jessica was a little raccoon. She was at an age in between being a baby and being a grown-up. She was sturdy and well-constructed, with a pointed nose and a little round stomach that jiggled whenever she laughed. She was usually happy. One morning though, she woke up slightly grouchy and sad. On this particular morning, she thought that she was too plain and ordinary. She wanted to be something special. She wanted to be magic.

She had begun to think about it early in the morning when

the sun first popped over the window sill. Every day, the sun lit up the sky. It helped the flowers grow and made the birds sing. It sparkled on the water and warmed Jessica's face. Everyone liked the sun. It was special. Jessica wanted to be special too.

Jessica's mother called her to breakfast at seven-thirty. Cereal again. Always cereal. Her father was so busy reading the newspaper at the breakfast table that he hardly even noticed Jessica.

"He'd notice me if I was magic," Jessica thought to herself. "I can't shine like the sun; but if I could go 'PUFF' and turn his newspaper into a lizard, he'd notice me then."

But Jessica couldn't go "PUFF" and turn a newspaper into a lizard. She thought about it for a moment. She even closed her eyes and whispered "PUFF" ever so softly under her breath to see what happened. But nothing happened. The newspaper stayed a newspaper; Jessica's father kept right on reading; and Jessica's cereal got soggy.

After breakfast, Jessica went out into the woods to play. "If I was a magic raccoon," she grumbled, "I'd go PUFF and turn the first berries I found into coins of silver and gold."

But turning berries into silver and gold is not something your average raccoon can do. Jessica wandered through the woods until she came to some berries. "PUFF," she shouted with more than a little annoyance and aggravation. But nothing happened. The berries stayed berries. They didn't look at all like silver or gold. Jessica ate them. They tasted sour.

The sun got hotter, and Jessica got grumpier. "I wish I was a magic raccoon,'" she said to herself again and again as she dragged on through the woods. "Then I'd be happy. Then people would notice me and know who I am."

"PUFF," she shouted at a chipmunk that scurried by. But the

chipmunk stayed a chipmunk. It didn't turn into a toad. "PUFF," she shouted at a babbling brook that ran past her. But the brook stayed a brook. It had no intention of turning into molasses.

It was the grumpiest raccoon ever who finally came to a stop by the tallest tree in the woods. "I'm so tired of being a plain, ordinary raccoon," she said to herself. "I'm not sure I'll ever be anything more than a plain old, ordinary raccoon."

That made things seem even worse. It was bad enough to be ordinary now. It was worse to be ordinary forever. Jessica slumped to the ground, and a tear drip-dropped down her cheek. "I wish I was a magic raccoon," she said. And then she began to cry softly to herself.

"Why are you crying, little raccoon?"

Jessica jumped.

"Why are you crying, little raccoon?" the voice asked again.

Jessica looked around. Standing beside her was a chipmunk. She wasn't sure, but she thought it might be the very same chipmunk she'd tried to turn into a toad a few minutes before.

"I'm crying because I'm just an ordinary raccoon," replied Jessica with her lower lip trembling. But now she was trying very hard not to cry, because she was embarrassed. "I'm crying because I wish I was magic."

"But you are magic," exclaimed the chipmunk. "Don't you understand?"

"No," replied Jessica. "I don't. I know I'm not magic. Just this morning, I tried to turn my father's newspaper into a lizard. I shouted PUFF but nothing happened. The newspaper stayed a newspaper. In the woods today, I tried to turn some berries into coins of silver and gold. I shouted PUFF but nothing happened. The berries stayed berries. I tried to turn the babbling brook into a stream of molasses. I shouted PUFF but nothing happened. And I'm a little ashamed to admit it, but I even tried to turn you into a toad. Nothing happened to you either, although I suppose I'm thankful for that. But it's very clear to me that I'm not magic."

"But you are magic, Jessica," said the chipmunk again. "Don't you understand? Look at all you did today. You took a walk in the woods. You stood in the sun. You saw red berries growing wild and ate them. You passed a sparkling blue brook that you can drink from when you're thirsty and cool off in when you're warm. You're alive. Life is beautiful! Life is the most beautiful magic of all."

Jessica wiped the tears from her eyes and thought for a moment. She felt very foolish now. The chipmunk was right. Magic wasn't going "PUFF" and turning things into lizards and toads. *REAL* magic was the magic of being alive.

And Jessica was very much alive. She had a cute pointed nose and a little round stomach that jiggled whenever she laughed. She had parents who loved her and gave her a home. She played in the woods every day. She ate wild berries when she was hungry, swam in the brook when she was hot, and drank its cold water when she was thirsty.

"You're right," Jessica told the chipmunk. "Thank you for showing me how foolish I've been." And with that, Jessica picked herself up, began to smile, and headed for home. She was very happy now. For she knew that, like all children everywhere, she had a little bit of magic in her. She was a magic raccoon.

ICE
CREAM
Rowena

# The Nasty, Mean, Greedy, Scary Flaggapoo Monster

*No more repulsive monster nor plague more cruel*
*Nor agent of heaven's anger more dire than this*
*Was ever thrust up from the Stygian waters.*

—*Virgil*

Once upon a time, in a deep, dark, dreary, faraway swamp, there lived a nasty, mean, greedy, scary flaggapoo monster. It was ten feet long with thick slimy skin, a long tail, short ugly legs, claws, beady red eyes, and a mouth full of the biggest, sharpest teeth anyone had ever seen. It had a nasty temper and was always hungry. But the flaggapoo monster was so mean and scary that all the other animals in the swamp kept far away. They wouldn't help it find anything to eat. And since it couldn't catch them to eat, the flaggapoo monster had to settle for swamp water for breakfast, swamp weeds for lunch, and swamp twigs for dinner.

With each passing day, the flaggapoo monster got hungrier and nastier. "I hate swamp water," it would say to itself. "I hate swamp weeds. I hate swamp twigs. I want something good to eat."

So one hot summer afternoon, the flaggapoo monster crawled out of its swamp to find something better to munch on. It crawled for several miles until it came to the edge of a forest. And there, a little bird was drinking from a pool of water.

"Ah hah," said the flaggapoo monster with a wicked grin. "Fresh poultry; just what I want for lunch."

So very very slowly and very very quietly, the nasty, mean, greedy, scary flaggapoo monster crawled up behind the little bird. . . . Its big jaws opened wide. . . . and began to snap shut. But just as the tremendous jaws were about to crunch tight, the little bird saw the flaggapoo monster's shadow. And just before the flaggapoo monster's jagged teeth crashed together, the little bird flew safely away to a nearby tree.

Well, you can imagine how angry and hungry the flaggapoo monster was now. In fact, it was so angry and hungry that it decided to crawl further away from the swamp than it was wise for any flaggapoo monster to go. On it went until it came to a big farm. And there, right in the middle of a cabbage patch, was the sweetest, plumpest rabbit the flaggapoo monster had ever seen.

Now, as a rule, rabbits are very much afraid of flaggapoo monsters. But this rabbit was so busy nibbling on cabbage that it didn't notice the flaggapoo monster sneaking up from behind. So very very slowly and very very quietly, the nasty, mean, greedy, scary flaggapoo monster crawled up behind the rabbit. Very quietly, it opened its big jaws wide and began to drool. And those terribly sharp teeth were all set to crunch down—when all of a sudden the same bird who had escaped moments before flew by and saw what was happening.

"Jump, rabbit, jump!" the bird shouted.

And then it happened. The flaggapoo monster's big jaws came crashing down. Its jagged teeth crashed together so hard that sparks flew. But thanks to the bird's warning, the rabbit hippity-hopped away with nothing missing but a patch of fur from its tail.

Now the nasty, mean, greedy, scary flaggapoo monster was angrier and hungrier than ever. So angry and hungry that steam began to rise from its nose. So angry and hungry that it crawled even further away from the swamp; further than any flaggapoo monster had ever gone before. Finally, it came to a road and stopped to rest. "I'm so hungry," the flaggapoo monster said to itself. "And I'm tired. I'm going to eat the very next thing that comes down this road."

So the nasty, mean, greedy, scary flaggapoo monster crawled out onto the middle of the road. It opened its jaws wide, and waited. Its big sharp teeth flashed a sly grin, and it said again, "I'm going to eat the very next thing that comes down this road."

Way off in the distance, there was a tinkling of bells. The nasty, mean, greedy, scary flaggapoo monster couldn't see exactly what was there, but it was coming closer.

"Dinner at last," it said with a smile. Then it opened its tremendous jaws even wider, flashed its big sharp teeth, and waited.

The bells came closer. Louder and louder they sounded until the flaggapoo monster could see what was there—a white ice cream truck. And as big as the nasty, mean, greedy, scary flaggapoo monster was, the ice cream truck was bigger. It had four big tires, a big white hood, and a very big freezer full of ice cream. But the flaggapoo monster had made up its mind.

"I'm going to eat the very next thing that comes down this road," it had decided. And that's exactly what it intended to do.

The ice cream truck came closer. But the nasty, mean, greedy, scary flaggapoo monster just stood there in the middle of the road with its jaws wide open and its big teeth flashing.

HONK, HONK . . . . The ice cream man blew his horn, but nothing happened. The nasty, mean, greedy, scary flaggapoo monster just stood there.

HONK, HONK . . . .

The flaggapoo monster wouldn't move.

HONK, HONK . . . HONK, HONK . . . .

**B O O M!**

The ice cream man jammed on his brakes, but it was too late. The flaggapoo monster looked like a pile of mashed potatoes.

"Stupid, old flaggapoo monster," the ice cream man said as he got out of his truck to look around. "It must have been a mean, greedy thing. I wonder what I should do with it. You don't see many flaggapoo monsters around these days."

Then the ice cream man got an idea. He picked up what was left of the flaggapoo monster, and put it in the back of his truck. From there, he drove into town and took the flaggapoo monster to a museum, where the curator promised to stuff it and put it on display. But before he drove off in his truck, the ice cream man had one favor to ask.

"Can I keep the nasty, mean, greedy, scary flaggapoo monster's teeth?"

"Why?" asked the museum curator.

"I want to make them into steak knives," the ice cream man told him.

Rowena

# Henry The Paintbrush

*"Glorious, stirring sight!" murmured Toad.*
*"O bliss! O poop-poop! O my! O my!"*

*—Kenneth Grahame*

Henry was as happy as a paintbrush could be the day Cathy brought him home from the store. Henry was Cathy's first paintbrush. And Cathy was Henry's first owner. Sometimes they'd just look at each other and smile.

Cathy was six years old, with skinny legs, lots of freckles, and reddish-brown hair. Henry was eight inches tall, with a wooden handle painted red and soft nylon bristles. Right away, Cathy gave Henry a place of his own on the corner of her workbench. From there, he could see Cathy's paint, stored in a thin metal box with six dried wells of color. . . . Red, orange, yellow, green, blue, and violet. And from there, Henry could look out the window at the sun and the sky.

Every day, Henry and Cathy would paint on sheets of smooth, white paper from a thick pad. They'd paint grass and flowers. They'd paint birds and trees. Cathy would dip Henry's bristles into a cup of water; then dab his head into the paint, and cover his bristles with color. Between colors, she'd dip Henry in the water again to wash him off. And when she was finished painting, she'd wash Henry one more time before brushing him dry on a paper towel and letting him rest for the night.

Henry loved Cathy, but after a while, he began to get a little bored. Cathy's paintings were pretty, but very ordinary. Her pictures of flowers and birds and trees and the sky weren't special enough to suit Henry.

"I wish I belonged to a famous artist," he said to himself one morning. "I wish I belonged to someone who created masterpiece paintings that hung in museums and people read about in magazines and newspapers."

Henry had heard about paintings like that. In fact, Cathy's family lived across the street from Pablo El Sloppo—one of the most famous painters in the world. El Sloppo paintings hung in museums in every country. People bought them for hundreds of thousand of dollars.

*One afternoon, Pablo El Sloppo came to visit Cathy and her parents.*

Henry could hear them talking in the living room.

"I am a famous painter," Pablo El Sloppo told Cathy. "I'm very rich, and I'm very important. Probably, I am the greatest painter of all time."

"And the most conceited," Henry thought to himself. "But I wish I could paint for an artist as famous as you."

For over an hour, Pablo El Sloppo kept bragging. Then he looked at Cathy and asked, "Would you like to see The Great El Sloppo at work?"

Cathy nodded.

"Very well, then. I have some paint and a canvas with me. Take me to a room with sunlight, and The Great El Sloppo will create a masterpiece for you."

Henry gulped. Cathy was bringing The Great Pablo El Sloppo into his room—right to Henry's workbench. As they came closer, Henry stared in awe.

Pablo El Sloppo was big and fat. His nose was shaped like a lightbulb. His hair was thick, black, and curly. A long, waxed moustache covered his face. One end of the moustache turned up; the other turned down. Henry thought he looked ridiculous, but maybe that was how famous artists were supposed to look.

Pablo El Sloppo put a piece of canvas on the workbench beside Henry. Next, he took a small glass palette, a wood-handled palette knife, and several tubes of oil paint from his smock pocket. Then he began to paint, smearing oil on the canvas with his palette knife. . . . Turquoise, black, and yukky orange.

"The perfect technique," he boasted to Cathy. "The perfect relationship of line to space . . . . The perfect blend of sight and color."

Henry looked on. The painting was ugly; a real mess. But Pablo El Sloppo was a famous artist. For sure, he had to know what he was doing.

"The perfect mix of dark and light. I am creating a masterpiece," bragged El Sloppo.

Cathy thought the painting was ugly too.

"At last, I am finished," El Sloppo announced. "Another work of genius by The Great Pablo El Sloppo. All I need to do now is put my signature on the canvas. And for that, I will need a paintbrush."

"Oh boy," thought Henry. "This is my chance to become famous."

Pablo El Sloppo looked around.

"Me!" cried Henry. "Me! Me! Me! Use me!"

Pablo El Sloppo reached out and took Henry in his fist.

"That brush isn't for oil—" Cathy started to say, but it was too late. Pablo El Sloppo had already stuffed Henry's head into a mound of thick black oil paint.

"I'm excited," thought Henry. "I'm scared, but I'm excited. I'm going to paint on real canvas with real oil paint in the hand of a master."

Pablo El Sloppo's hand was much bigger than Cathy's; so large that it was a little scary for Henry. The oil paint was thicker and heavier than the water colors Henry was used to. It had a strong greasy smell that was beginning to give him a headache. The canvas was rough; very different from Cathy's smooth,white paper. Henry was starting to get scrapes and bruises.

Pablo El Sloppo finished painting his signature.

"My masterpiece is complete," he told Cathy and her parents. "Now you must give me a sandwich, because I am hungry."

"I don't feel good," Henry thought to himself. "My headache is getting worse."

Pablo El Sloppo threw Henry down on the workbench. "Right now! I must eat immediately."

Cathy and her parents led Pablo El Sloppo out of the workroom and into the kitchen. Henry could hear their voices in the distance. "I *really* don't feel good," he said to himself. "My head hurts. I'm covered with slimy oil paint. My bristles are getting hard. Maybe if I wriggle around a little, I'll—"

Henry tried moving his bristles, but they were stiff.

"Try harder," he told himself. "Push!"

They wouldn't move.

"Omigosh! This is awful! I can't move! I'm paralyzed!"

The slimy oil paint was starting to harden.

"Help!" Henry shouted. "Somebody, help!"

The smell was worse. He couldn't breathe.

"Help, please!"

Henry's eyes were stuck shut. He was beginning to choke and gasp for air.

"Help," he moaned. "Help!" But it was no use. He was growing weak. No one could hear. He was getting dizzy. Everything was a blur.

"Arggh . . . . arggh . . . . "

And then, just when Henry was about to lapse into unconsciousness, he heard Cathy calling. And the next thing he knew, she was holding him in her arms, saying, "You poor little paintbrush. Don't worry. I'll take care of you."

Very carefully, Cathy poured some turpentine into a cup. She dipped Henry in, swished him around, and pulled him out to wipe his bristles on a gentle cloth. Then she did it again. . . . And again. . . . Three. . . Four . . . . Five times. Next, she filled another cup with warm water, and dipped Henry in for a final bath. After that, she wiped his bristles clean on a paper towel and stood him up by the window in the sunlight to dry.

Henry slept well that night. He was very tired. And as he slept, he began to dream . . . . Pleasant dreams . . . . He dreamt about all the flowers and trees he'd paint with Cathy in the days to come. He dreamt about how he and Cathy would paint simple everyday things like birds and grass and clouds and the sky.

Rowena

# Jonathan Gobble

*We hold these truths to be self-evident, that all Men are created equal, that they are endowed by their Creator with certain unalienable Rights, that among these are Life, Liberty, and the pursuit of Happiness. That to secure these rights, Governments are instituted among Men, deriving their just Powers from the consent of the governed. That whenever any Form of Government becomes destructive of these ends, it is the Right of the People to alter or abolish it. . . .*

*—The Declaration of Independence*

Jonathan Gobble was a funny looking turkey. His head was tiny and shaped like the head of a pin. His body was plump with three brown feathers sticking out of his tail. His legs were long and boney with little feet hardly big enough for balance. His beak was orange. His eyes were brown. Jonathan's neck was long and skinny. He had a big Adam's apple that bounced up and down when he ran and popped in and out when he talked. When Jonathan Gobble ran and talked at the same time, his Adam's apple bounced and popped all over the place.

Jonathan lived a long time ago. He was born in 1773 on a small farm in Pennsylvania. His owners, Silas and Sarah Adams, lived on the same farm, which was near a dark green forest and a little town with no name.

Once every week, Silas and Sarah would drive their horse and wagon into town for supplies. Whenever they went, Jonathan ran with them. His tiny feet would fly down the road as the horse and wagon clippity-clopped ahead. And as he ran, Jonathan would call to the birds and chatter to the flowers and trees, with his Adam's apple bouncing up and down and popping in and out all over the place.

Jonathan liked going to town. But one trip was always special. Once a month, every month, all the townspeople would gather together for a town meeting. These meetings were very important, because it was there that they made the decisions that governed their lives. They would discuss what to do about clearing a road to the next community and how to set up a school to educate their children. They talked about getting water from the nearby creek and the best way to prepare for the cold hard winter ahead. Every person, from the mayor to the man who ran the general store, had one vote. And when each meeting came to a close, the townspeople followed the will of the majority.

By the time Jonathan Gobble was three, he was a very well-known turkey. As a matter of fact, everyone in town knew Jonathan. It wasn't simply that he was the funniest looking turkey any of the townsfolk had ever seen. It wasn't even that Jonathan was the only turkey who trotted into town every week alongside his owner's horse and wagon, calling to the birds and chattering to the flowers and trees. The most noticeable aspect of Jonathan Gobble's behavior was the way he attended town meetings. Whatever the subject of discussion, Jonathan would stand perfectly still behind the last row of chairs in the town hall. His tiny little feet would hold him perfectly erect, and his Adam's apple wouldn't move at all. He would listen quietly; and as each person spoke, Jonathan's eyes never wavered from the speaker. At times, a sense of intelligence, dignity, and even pride shone in Jonathan Gobble's face as he watched the town meeting at work.

By the time Jonathan was three though, the town meetings had begun to change. Less and less time was spent discussing local schools and the nearby creek. Far fewer hours passed in debate on clearing roads and preparation for the long hard winter ahead. The year was 1776, and the townspeople began to talk of far-away places like Boston and Philadelphia. They began to speak of men named Washington and Jefferson and a King who lived in a land called England.

For the first time now, the townspeople were divided. Many of them joined with Silas and Sarah Adams in voicing support for a Declaration of Independence which had been written in Philadelphia that very year. However, others spoke just as forcefully in defense of the King.

On a bright sunny day in the summer of 1776, the people of the little town with no name met for their most important town meeting ever. The raging debate between the men who signed the Declaration of Independence and the King of England had broken into war in a place called Massachusetts. All across the colonies of America, men and women were being called upon to take sides. The people of the little town with no name had to choose.

The town meeting began shortly after noon, with Jonathan Gobble standing perfectly still behind the last row of chairs in the town hall. Silas Adams was the first to speak, and as he talked of freedom and independence, Jonathan's chest filled with pride. Sarah Adams spoke next, and Jonathan's eyes brimmed with tears as she spoke of liberty and the pursuit of happiness. One after another, the town doctor, the man who ran the general store, and the town mayor spoke in defense of the right of people to be free. But those who supported the King had not yet had their say. At last, Charles Curtis—the wealthiest farmer in the little town with no name—rose to speak.

"Get that stupid turkey out of here," said Charles Curtis.

Jonathan Gobble blinked.

"Get that stupid turkey out of here," Charles Curtis said again. "This is a serious meeting. I'm not going to discuss the future of this community and the fate of the entire colony with a dumb turkey in the room."

Jonathan couldn't believe his ears.

"You'd better put your turkey outside," the mayor told Silas Adams. "I don't think he's doing any harm. He's been coming to town meetings for three years and never caused a fuss. But for the sake of an orderly meeting, we had best proceed without him."

Silas walked to the back of the room and patted Jonathan gently on top of his tiny head. "I'm sorry," he said as he led Jonathan from the room. "The mayor says I have to put you outside."

As Silas left him on the town hall porch, a lump slowly rose in Jonathan's throat. It clogged his skinny neck and got all tangled up with his Adam's apple. The tears streamed down Jonathan's cheeks, and he cried without shame. The most important town meeting in the history of the little town with no name was going on, and Jonathan Gobble, who hadn't missed a town meeting in three years, wasn't allowed inside.

As the hours passed, the afternoon sun grew warmer. Jonathan dried his tears, and pressed an ear to the town hall wall so he could hear the debate inside. Charles Curtis was still speaking, his loud voice bellowing through the hall.

A bright patch of red flashed through the dark green forest leaves.

Jonathan squinted and looked into the distance.

There it was again. Far away on the other side of the forest, two long lines of soldiers in bright red uniforms were marching toward the town.

"Omigosh," thought Jonathan as the soldiers made their way down the mountainside. "Omigosh," he said out loud as they came into closer view. "Omigosh! The British are coming. The British Are Coming! *The British are coming!"* shouted Jonathan Gobble as he raced back into the town hall. *"The British are coming! The British are coming!"*

Charles Curtis was in midsentence when Jonathan charged back into the meeting squawking at the top of his lungs.

"Stop that racket," shouted Charles Curtis.

*"The British are coming!"* squawked Jonathan Gobble. *"The British are coming!"*

He was very excited and no one could understand him, but the urgency of his cry was enough to spur the townsfolk to action.

Silas and the mayor raced to the window, and saw the two long lines of red soldiers off in the distance. "The British are coming," shouted the mayor.

"We can stop them," cried the town doctor.

"Follow me," shouted the man who ran the general store, as

he led the townsfolk to the front of the store and began passing out rifles and ammunition.

The battle that followed was short. The British had hoped to catch the townsfolk unaware, but the men and women of the little town with no name were ready for them. The British surrendered after less than an hour of fighting.

There were many heroes in battle that afternoon. Silas Adams fought bravely in the front line. The town doctor cared for those who were wounded, and Sarah Adams carried water to those who were thirsty. The man who ran the general store handed out supplies, and the town mayor directed the fighting.

The biggest hero of all though, was the watchman who warned the townsfolk of their danger. His statue stands today, two hundred years later, in front of the town hall he helped to protect. The little town is now named after him. You can see the statue for yourself if you ever pass through Gobblesburg, Pennsylvania.

Rowena

# The Little Evergreen Tree

*Merry Christmas! What right have you to be merry? What reason have you to be merry? You're poor enough.*

*—Charles Dickens*

High on the side of Lookout Mountain, the little evergreen tree stood alone. The winter sun had dropped beneath the horizon, and all around there was night. An icy wind whipped at the little evergreen's branches and raged ferociously down the mountainside. December 24th, the day before Christmas, was about to end. Darkness reigned.

The little evergreen tree had been born in promise. Years before, it had been sown on the side of Lookout Mountain. It had sprouted in the spring amidst a host of bright green seedlings. As the seasons passed, a forest grew. Delicate shafts turned to awkward stalks, and then to rangy saplings. Year after year, the trees matured until finally there grew on the side of Lookout Mountain a forest of the tallest, proudest trees in the land.

But the little evergreen didn't grow with them. The other trees grew taller. Their branches reached for the sky, and as they did, they cut the little evergreen off from the warm rays of the sun. Their roots dug deeper, and as they stretched into the soil, they robbed the little evergreen of the nourishment it needed to grow. Life was a daily struggle. With every passing season, the other trees grew taller, fuller, and prouder. The little evergreen grew weary and worn. Its branches thinned, and its narrow spine weakened as it fought to survive.

In early December, after years of waiting, Farmer Brown opened the side of Lookout Mountain and put his trees on sale. From all over the land, people came to buy. Farmer Brown's trees were the finest in the nation, and no self-respecting bank or major corporation would be without one.

The man from Wadsworth Bank, located at One Wadsworth Plaza, was the first to come. "Only the biggest and best of Farmer Brown's evergreen trees for Wadsworth Bank," he said, as he took a wad of money from his pocket and began to peel off hundred-dollar bills. An hour later, the man from Wadsworth Bank was gone, taking with him the tallest, finest, fullest evergreen tree on Lookout Mountain.

The man from Conglomeration, Inc. was next. "Only the second biggest and second best of Farmer Brown's evergreen trees for Conglomeration, Inc.," he said, as he took a slightly smaller wad of money from his pocket and began to peel off fifty-dollar bills. An hour later, the man from Conglomeration, Inc. was gone. The second tallest, second finest, second fullest evergreen tree on Lookout Mountain went with him.

So it went, day after day. People came, paid their money, and left. Slowly, the forest thinned. The little evergreen tree went unnoticed. The day before Christmas, the last of the other trees was sold. The little evergreen stood alone.

The tree at Wadsworth Bank, located at One Wadsworth Plaza, was beyond a doubt the most lavishly decorated Christmas tree in the land. From the moment it rolled into the big city on the back of a giant trailer truck, it was the center of attention. A dozen men with blocks and pulleys hoisted it from the trailer and stood it upright in the center of the plaza. A dozen more of Wadsworth Bank's most trusted employees hung strands of gold from its giant boughs and streamed colored lights across its branches. A choir of sixty schoolchildren in red and white robes sang carols at its side. And three uniformed security men stood guard round the clock lest someone try in any way to mar its haughty splendor.

The tree at Conglomeration, Inc. was beyond a doubt the second most lavishly decorated Christmas tree of any in the land. When it arrived, ten men, grunting and groaning, lifted it from the truck and stood it upright in the center of the plaza. They were joined by ten more of Conglomeration, Inc.'s most trusted employees, who hung strands of silver from its giant boughs and decked its limbs with Christmas ornaments. A choir of fifty schoolchildren in green and white robes sang Christmas carols by its side. And two uniformed security men stood guard round the clock lest someone try to do it harm.

All across the land, the trees from Farmer Brown's mountain were royally adorned. In banks and prestigious universities, in brokerage houses and corporate headquarters, they were trimmed in the grandest splendor imaginable. No expense was too great; no effort was spared. After all, Christmas might not be Christmas without a very large, very fine, very lavishly decorated Christmas tree for people to crowd around.

Farmer Brown's trees proudly wore their finery with a grandeur befitting trees that towered to the sky.

Christmas Eve was very cold and dark on Lookout Mountain. The winter wind howled ferociously as it cascaded down the mountainside. It tore savagely at the little evergreen's branches, and icy tears trickled from the little evergreen's eyes. Without the taller trees to protect it from the cold, the little evergreen doubted its ability to survive.

The sound of footsteps echoed in the night.

A lantern and one, two, three heads bobbed into view, as Farmer Brown made his way up the mountain with his son and daughter at his side.

"They didn't leave much," said Farmer Brown. "Just the little evergreen tree. It's just as well, though. I always liked the little evergreen best."

Farmer Brown and his two children carried heavy shovels. As the wind grew in intensity, they surrounded the little evergreen and began to dig.

"Careful now," Farmer Brown cautioned. "We don't want to hurt its roots. Make sure you dig deeply enough into the soil so we can lift the little evergreen out without any harm."

When the digging stopped, they slipped a rope around the little evergreen's branches. Then, very carefully, they lifted it onto their shoulders and carried it back to the farmhouse where they lived.

It was warm inside the house, and the scent of homemade pies filled the air. A cheery glow danced among the logs in the fireplace, and the howl of the icy wind seemed far away. Farmer Brown's son set the little evergreen on end in a huge oak bucket in the center of the living room. Then, very gently, he began to pack loose dirt around the base of its trunk.

"Make sure the roots are protected," Farmer Brown told him. "After the new year begins, we'll want to replant the little evergreen right by the farmhouse door. That way, it will be with us for many Christmases to come."

When the little evergreen tree was snug and warm in the oak bucket, Farmer Brown's daughter took a string of pine cones she had gathered from the forest floor and wrapped them gently around its fragile branches. Farmer Brown's wife brought a large box of handmade ornaments into the living room. The ornaments had been handed down from generation to generation. For over fifty years, the Brown family had added one new ornament to the box every Christmas.

One by one, the children hung the Christmas ornaments on the little evergreen's branches. At the very top, Farmer Brown put the star. Then the children and their parents laid their presents under the little evergreen and went to sleep. As the hour of midnight approached, the little evergreen tree was surrounded by warmth and love.

Christmas day dawned windy and cold in the big cities. At Wadsworth Bank, located at One Wadsworth Plaza, an icy wind raged ferociously through the caverns created by tall monstrous buildings on either side. At Conglomeration, Inc., the dawn was bleak and gray. All across the land, people gathered in the warmth of their churches and homes. Outside the banks and corporations, at the prestigious universities and brokerage houses, the once proud, towering trees that had grown on Lookout Mountain faced Christmas Day cold and alone.